Hector the Spectre

Jana Hunter

Illustrated by
Mike Gordon

PUFFIN BOOKS

PUFFIN BOOKS

Published by the Penguin Group
Penguin Books Ltd, 27 Wrights Lane, London W8 5TZ, England
Penguin Books USA Inc., 375 Hudson Street, New York, New York 10014, USA
Penguin Books Australia Ltd, Ringwood, Victoria, Australia
Penguin Books Canada Ltd, 10 Alcorn Avenue, Toronto, Ontario, Canada M4V 3B2
Penguin Books (NZ) Ltd, 182–190 Wairau Road, Auckland 10, New Zealand

Penguin Books Ltd, Registered Offices: Harmondsworth, Middlesex, England

First published by Viking 1993
Published in Puffin Books 1994
1 3 5 7 9 10 8 6 4 2

Printed in England by Clays Ltd, St Ives plc

Contents

Hector Goes
to School

It is midnight in the city.
   Alone, at the top of a very
creepy stone tower . . .

Hector the Spectre is in high spirits.

Telling jokes is Hector's favourite game. Hector the Spectre is a ghost with a dream. A dream to be a comedian. Now that's a dream just perfect for you or me. But for a ghost . . .

being funny is a TOTAL DISASTER!

But Hector is not *like* other ghosts.

Hector prefers jaunts to
haunts . . .

quips to crypts . . .

and comic turns to stomach
churns.

In fact, Hector's parents
despair of him ever being a
proper ghost. They have to
admit that as a spectre . . .

Hector is hopeless!

GHOUL SCHOOL REPORT

Name **Hector**   Age **100**

SUBJECT	COMMENTS	GRADE
SPOOKING TESTS	Hector prefers fooling to ghouling.	1/20
HAUNTING	No life in him!	0/100
EXORCIZES	Never does his moanwork	2/100
REELING WRITHING	Hasn't the ghost of a chance	2/100
SCARESTIFF-MATIC		0/100
INVISIBLE WRITING		

A very disappointing century for Hector. He dreams instead of screams. What's worse - he dreams of being a comic! Unheard of!   *S. Scarem*

HEAD SCREECHER

"Hector, your final Ghoul School report is dreadful," Dad groans.

14

"Don't look so *grave*, Dad," Hector giggles.

"Stop it, Hector," Dad says. "You know proper ghosts don't tell jokes."

"Or speak with their mouths
in a smile," adds Mum.
"Sorry I spook,"
quips Hector.

Dad sighs. "I'm afraid
there's only one person who
can stop him fooling. This is a
job for . . .

17

"the Spectre Inspector! He's the expert at making ghosts scary."

The Spectre Inspector flies to
the rescue . . .

"Inspector, please make our
son scary," begs Mum.

"If you can," adds Dad.

20

"Hee hee," laughs Hector.

The Inspector promises to
follow Hector and stop his
jokes.

For days the Inspector tails Hector.

He stalks him and stops him.

He trails him and traps him.

He turns up in the oddest places.

But Hector is not discouraged.

The Inspector tells Hector's parents, "Hector's the worst case I've had this century . . . there's only one place that might cure him."

"The creepy crypt?" offers
Dad.

"The dank dungeon?"
whispers Mum.

"The *stage*?" shouts Hector
hopefully.

"No, not the crypt, not the dungeon, and *definitely* not the stage," says the Inspector sternly. "But . . .

32

"*Windy End School!*"

"Windy End Schooool?" echoes Mum. "But those Windy End kids aren't afraid of anything!"

"Exactly! If Hector learns to scare them he'll be a proper ghost."

"It's your last chance, Hector," says Dad. "Scare those kids or it's back to Ghoul School for you."

Hector hates Ghoul School, but
he loves being around kids,
so for a while he does his best.

35

But being scary isn't nearly so much fun

as making people laugh.
Until . . .

something catches Hector's eye . . .

and he doesn't wait to be
invited.

In no time Hector is the star of the show.

Why did the ghost get expelled from school?

Because he was a little terror!

His jokes have the Windy End
kids screaming with laughter.

Mum, Dad and the Inspector are so thrilled to hear the noises coming from Windy End that they don't stop to find out why.

Little do they know that the Windy End kids, thrilled to have their own comic ghost, beg Hector to stay.

At last Hector is a ghost who's
got his dream. A dream to do
nothing but jest.

For Hector thinks of all the
screams . . . screams of
laughter are the best!

45

Dear Inspector

   Thank you for curing Hector. He is now resident ghost at Windy End School. Every day the shrieks coming from the school prove Hector's the <u>scariest</u> ghost around.

                    Hector's
                  Mum & Dad

Hector Visits the Fair

The Windy Enders are at it again. It's the school trip to Crumblingum Castle.

Everyone is wild with excitement (especially Hector – he's never been on a school trip).

Crumblingum Castle has turrets and towers, a drawbridge and dungeons. It's even rumoured to have ghosts.

Hector hoots. He is much
more interested in fun than
fear, and in the castle grounds
is the famous Crumblingum
fun-fair. Hector has dreamed
of fairs for centuries. (He's
dying to try
the rides.)

I'll make things go
bump in the night...
the dodgems!

Now he can't wait a moment
longer.

But at Crumblingum Castle
they are greeted by a bellow
like the snort of a disgruntled
rhino.

SILENCE!

It's Gilda Glump, Crum-
blingum Castle's guide. The
Glump has been spoiling school
trips for years. She knows just
how to dampen the excitement
of any child. She does not
believe in fooling around. She

does not believe in fairs *or fun* either! In fact, she does not believe in anything much except work and yelling her head off.

In no time The Glump has
every Windy Ender wearing
their pencil to a stub.

Hector is bored witless. He is reminded of Ghoul School. Every Monday at Ghoul School was Castle Haunting . . . a whole night of it. Hector hated it. But the memory of those ghastly nights gives him a great idea. And soon he is up to his old tricks.

Coooooeee!

He heckles and hides.

He burrows and blows.

He disappears in the strangest ways. Until even The Glump is rattled.

While deep deep down in the
creepiest castle crypt,
something stirs . . .
GHOSTS!

Bad-tempered ghosts, who
hate to be awakened. They are
the ghosts of the ancient
Crumb family led by Lord
Crumb III, the most miserable
of them all. (He wasn't much
fun in life either.) Lord Crumb,
though dead for 200 years, still
thinks he owns the place.

"We must find the intruder,"
Crumb moans, "and stop his
nonsense."

The Crumb ghosts flap about
the castle like demented bats.
Bats out for blood . . .
determined to catch their prey.
And their prey is . . .
HECTOR!

The Crumb ghosts are so shocked by Hector's jokes that before you can say *quivering ectoplasm* they whisk him down, down, down to the darkest dungeon.

"Stay here," orders Lord Crumb. "Haunt," he moans. "Or else!"

Left alone, Hector tries to cheer himself up by being funny.

Moan, moan, moan. That's all they ever do!

Wish I could vault this vault.

Just call me the remains who remains!

Ha ha!

But trapped in the dungeon with ghost guards at every wall, Hector sees his chances of fun at the fair vanish into thin air. UNTIL . . .

A familiar loud snort echoes down the stone steps.

TAPESTRY

A snort like the bellow of a disgruntled rhino. A rhino on the rampage.

Suddenly Hector is hopeful. He knows that even the gravest grump has a funny bone somewhere. And before the Glump has time to grunt, Hector's thrown a tapestry over her head.

So, between the Glump's
gulps and guffaws . . . between
her giggles and gasps . . .
Hector makes his get-away . . .

with the Windy Enders . . .
to the fair!

But little does Hector know, the Crumb ghosts have sent for Hector's old adversary . . . THE SPECTRE INSPECTOR!

The Spectre Inspector stalks
the fairground in search of
Hector . . . always just one
ride behind. Only to catch up
with him in the GHOST TRAIN!

And it's here the Inspector is
so completely fooled that
Hector is finally left to have
fun in peace.

My favourite ride... the roller

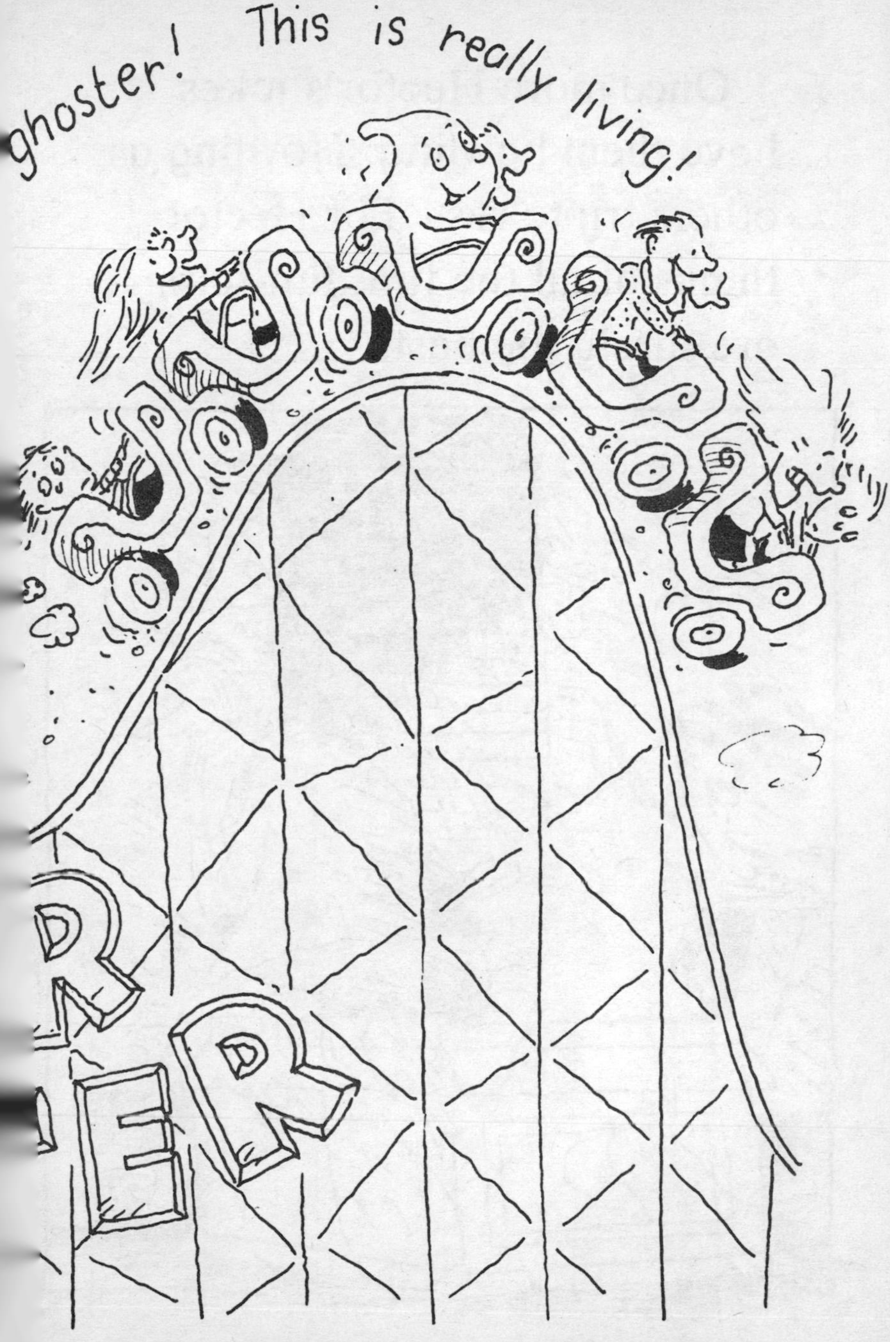
ghoster! This is really living!

Once more Hector's jokes
have them howling. Howling as
others try to rest. For Hector
thinks of all the fun, fun-fairs
are surely the best!

Dear Hector

Keep up the good work at Windy End. Dad and I are proud of you.

Love
Mum

PS The Inspector is busy with a new case - a Missing Ghost with the bellow of a disgruntled rhino. Have you seen it?